THE PINK BALLOON

WRITTEN BY
NANCY SHEA

For Linden, Paisley and Sutton,
whose hearts were screened
for super powers.
Of course they all have them.

May your mom's
grace and courage
inspire you always.

Katie was always happy. She lived in a happy little house.
Her mom was happy too. Her dad was happy. Her brothers were happy.
Her baby sister was happy. Even her two puppies were happy.

Katie loved to dance.
She loved to swing.
She loved flowers
and sunshine.

She even loved rain. That was because she loved her raincoat and her shiny rain boots. She loved the sound that the rain made on her umbrella; tap...tap...tap... like music from the sky.

One day, Katie went to see Dr. Heather with her mom. Dr. Heather was a Heart Doctor. She had very curly hair and a kind face. Katie loved Dr. Heather's hair.

Dr. Heather was very serious today. She told Katie and her mom that Katie had a problem with her heart. She could take medicine to help her heart, but she would have to be careful. She would have to be careful when she danced. She would be tired.

"Why? I always eat my
vegetables, I always get
fresh air and sunshine. I
have a bath every day, and
I always brush my teeth."
Katie didn't understand.

"You did everything right, but sometimes these things just happen," Dr. Heather answered softly. "We will take care of this."

Katie was not happy anymore. Her mom was not happy either. They walked slowly out of the office. The sun was shining, but it was not a happy day.

On the way home, they walked by a store that had balloons in the window. Katie's mom asked her, "Would you like a nice pink balloon? One that is shaped like a heart? Maybe that would make you feel better."

Katie didn't think so, but the balloon was pretty so she nodded her head. The balloon blew high in the sky and danced merrily in the breeze. It did make her feel better!

Every day after that, Katie's mom tied the balloon on Katie's wrist so it wouldn't blow away. The balloon went everywhere with her. To the park....to school... to the grocery store...

Everywhere!

Dr. Heather was right; Katie did feel tired. While Katie was walking home from the park one day, feeling especially tired, she saw a little boy sitting on the steps of his house. He looked very sad. "Are you sad today?" Katie asked. The boy didn't say anything, just nodded.

"Here!" she said joyfully. "I was sad too, but this balloon made me feel better. Maybe it will make you feel better too!" The boy smiled. His smile grew bigger, and it made Katie smile too. She skipped all the way home.

"Why Katie, where is your balloon?" her mom asked when she came in the door. Katie responded gleefully. "I saw a little boy. He was sad, so I gave him my balloon. He feels better, and so do I."

Katie's mom was proud. So, the next day when they walked to the store, she bought Katie another balloon. But on the way home, they saw a man walking with his hands in his pockets, and he didn't look very happy.

"Here!" Katie said cheerily, and she put the balloon's ribbon around the man's wrist. The balloon danced in the breeze. The man smiled, and Katie smiled.

The next day, Katie's mom bought her two balloons. This time, they didn't even make it to the end of the street before Katie had given her balloons to a lady on a bench at the bus stop, and a little girl who had skinned her knee on the sidewalk.

Katie's mom started to buy pink heart balloons every day now. Katie's brothers and sister had balloons in their rooms too. The man in the store had to put more pink heart balloons in the window. Soon, the whole store was full of pink heart balloons.

And then,
an amazing thing happened.

Katie and her pink balloons had inspired others to share comfort and hope. The boy on the front steps was visiting the man in the store every day, and giving balloons to people that he thought needed to feel better.

The man with his hands
in his pockets was sharing
balloons too. Soon, people
all over the town were
sharing comfort and
hope by carrying pink
heart balloons and
giving them away.

Katie and her mom walked down the street and saw the boy from the front steps with his balloon. They saw the man with his hands in his pockets with his balloon. There were more people with balloons. There were balloons everywhere!

Katie knew, with all these balloons spreading hope and cheering for her, that everything was going to be fine.

And it was.

From left to right:
Elizabeth Halka,
Katie Shea
Nancy Shea

"It's all in the genes." - Dr. Heather Ross

The next generation

FriesenPress

Suite 300 - 990 Fort St
Victoria, BC, V8V 3K2
Canada

www.friesenpress.com

ISBN
978-1-5255-8791-7 (Hardcover)
978-1-5255-8790-0 (Paperback)
978-1-5255-8792-4 (eBook)

*1. Juvenile Fiction, Health & Daily Living, Diseases,
Illnesses & Injuries*

Distributed to the trade by The Ingram Book Company